FROM A TO Z001

an amazing journey filled with wonder and wisdom
for the young and young at heart

created by
Margaret David Laborde
and Rebecca Feeney Doherty

illustrated by
Paul Kalil Roach

Margaret dedicates this book to her son, Collins, whose creative intuition and vision have been a constant source of inspiration. "My life has been blessed by your presence in it, and I love you more than words can say! May your life be filled with joy and wonder, and may all of your dreams come true!" –Mom

Rebecca dedicates this book to her amazing granddaughters, Annabelle and Miriam, whom she loves to the moon and moon and moon and back again. "May you always reach for the moon because that is the only way you can catch a star. And may all of your dreams come true!" –Oh-Ma B

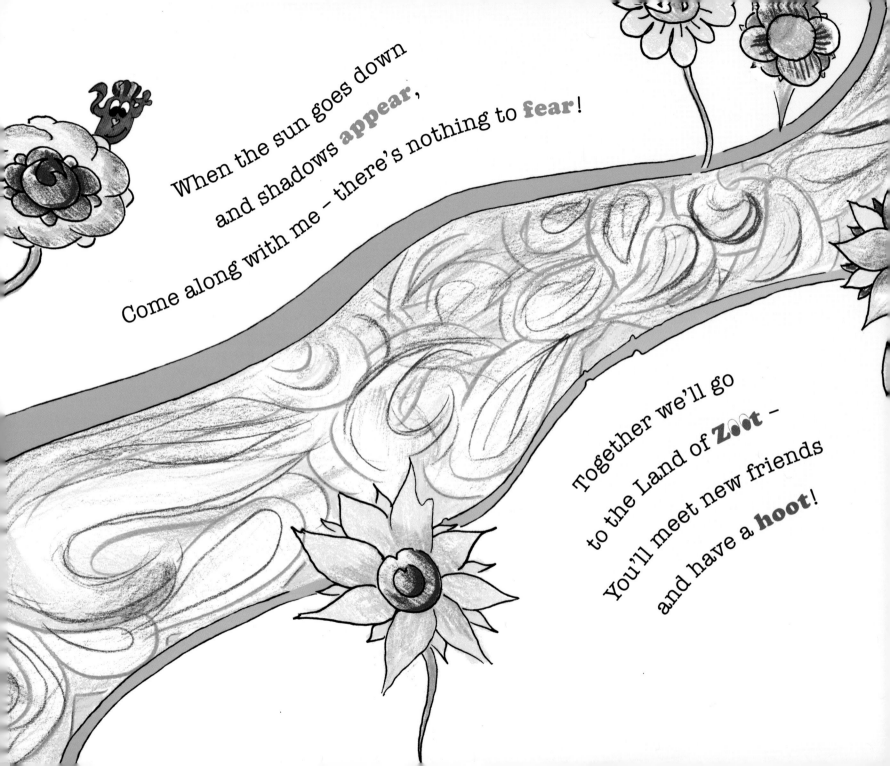

When the sun goes down
and shadows **appear**,
Come along with me – there's nothing to **fear**!

Together we'll go
to the Land of **Zoot** –
You'll meet new friends
and have a **hoot**!

We'll play a game
at every **stage**.

Try to find me on
every **page**!

Just climb up the apple, slide
down the **chute**, and. . .

Step into the magical
Land of **Z⦿⦿t**!

Aa

An Accepting Alligator will recognize,

That a good friend comes in any size.

Bb

A Brilliant Butterfly
flutters with **fun**,

Exploring each day,
one by **one**.

Cc

A Creative Cricket
sings his own **song**,

Inspiring the world
to sing right **along**.

Dd

A Daring Dolphin
dreams ever so **high**,

Searching for gems
way up in the **sky**.

Ee

An Enchanted Elf
peeks out from a **tree**,

Looking at all
there is to **see**.

Ff

A Fun-loving Fairy
is often **spied**,

With a friendly dragonfly,
hitching a **ride**.

Gg

A Gracious Giraffe
standing high **above**,

Bends down to gently
guide those she **loves**.

Hh

A Happy Hare
with a grateful **heart**,

Counts his blessings
each day, at the **start**.

Ii

An Itty-bitty Inchworm
at a measured pace,

Inches forward
with a smile on his face

Jj

A Joyful Jellyfish
goes with the **flow**,

Enjoying life's journey
at high tide and **low**.

Kk

A Kind-hearted King
with respect for **all**,

Invites animals to dance
at his very grand **ball**.

L1

A Lucky Ladybug with good fortune to **bring**,

Grants wishes to all who wish a good **thing**!

Mm

A Mindful Mermaid
who cares about **others**,

Always supports her
sisters and **brothers**.

Nn

A Noble Newt
who likes to **play**,

Creates magic in
his own special **way**.

Oo

An Observant Owl
sits up in a **tree**,

Hooting his wisdom
for you and for **me**.

Pp

A Plucky Peacock,
so happy and **free**,

Shows her inner beauty
for all to **see**!

A Quiet Queen
goes out on a limb,

To stand up for what
she truly believes in.

Rr

A Rugged Rhinoceros
with strength and **power**,

Pauses to sniff
a delicate **flower**.

Ss

A Sharing Seahorse
prances **along**,

Giving rides to those
who are not as **strong**.

Tt

A Traveling Turtle
roams far and **wide**,

Gathering life lessons
and storing them **inside**.

Uu

A Unique Unicorn
flies far into **space**,

To explore and discover
every new **place**.

Vv

A Valentine Vole
with love to **share**,

Shows others how much
she truly **cares**.

Ww

A Winged Warthog
seeking no **fame**,

Spreads joy and wonder
with her enchanting **cane**.

Xx

An eX-traordinary X
knows where treasure
is **found**:

A chest of wonder tucked
deep in the **ground**.

Yy

A Youthful Yak
with a heart of gold,

Welcomes all he meets
on his colorful road.

Zz

And the last is the first,
surely you **see**?

For it's a Z👀tsnoot...
Yes! It's **Me**!

And now that our journey
must come to an **end**,

Get back to the place
that you've already **been**.

Climb right up the apple,
then slide on **down**—

Slide right back into
your very own **town**!

Now sleep well, my friend,
and never fear.

Your next visit
can be ever so near!

For the Land of Zoot,
once visited and seen,

Can always be found in
the hearts of you and me!

Sweet Dreams...

Rebecca is a senior U.S. District Court Judge and former teacher. Every day since her grandchildren were born, she has read them a good night story, and she wanted to create the perfect book for their shared nightly journey—one that invites all to visit a magical kingdom, populated by endearing creatures who share gentle life lessons and inspire the unlimited possibilities of the imagination.

Margaret is an attorney from Louisiana. It is Margaret's genuine belief that the words we choose to describe ourselves and our world shape our behavior and, ultimately, our lives. This core belief was lovingly woven throughout *From A to Zoot* to gently encourage positive thinking and an appreciation for the goodness and wonder all around us.

Photo by Nathan Francis

Paul is a gifted young artist from New Orleans, Louisiana, and has chosen to hone his skills in studio art at Loyola University. Paul has captured the wonderful whimsy of imagination and brought it to life on the printed page.

Photo by Cynthia Sparks